This Little Tiger book belongs to:

_____

_____

_____

_____

For the magic in my life: Mark, Joe, Jess and James

~ J H

For Rhiannon, my fairy goddaughter

~ A E

LITTLE TIGER PRESS
An imprint of Magi Publications
1 The Coda Centre, 189 Munster Road,
London SW6 6AW
www.littletigerpress.com

First published in Great Britain 2011
This edition published 2011

Text copyright © Julia Hubery 2011
Illustrations copyright © Alison Edgson 2011
Julia Hubery and Alison Edgson have asserted their rights to be
identified as the author and illustrator of this work under the
Copyright, Designs and Patents Act, 1988

A CIP catalogue record for this book is
available from the British Library

Printed in China

LTP/1800/0194/1110

2 4 6 8 10 9 7 5 3 1

A Little Fairy Magic

Julia Hubery   *   Alison Edgson

LITTLE TIGER PRESS
London

Phoebe was fizzing with excitement in her new fairy costume. She loved her shimmery wings and her floaty pink dress.

"Look at my wings! Look at my starry wand!" she squeaked, twirling and whirling.

"Now I'm a real, real fairy!" she sang, as she spun and danced.

"You're a fairy princess," smiled Daddy, "and you need an enchanted castle. Come and look . . ."

Phoebe peeped into her bedroom.

"Wow!" she whispered.

Her bedroom sparkled with stars
and twinkles and silvery sprinkles.

"Make us some magic, Phoebe,"
said her big brother Sam.

"I'm going to fly first!" said Phoebe.

She raced into the garden and scrambled up on to the old tree stump.

"I will fly just like a fairy," she thought.

She stood on tiptoes, and stretched her arms.

She leapt high into the air,
waving her wand . . .

. . . and landed BUMP! in the flower bed.

"Oh dear," sighed Phoebe,
"maybe flying is too hard for
a brand new fairy – I'll practise
wishes instead."

She decided to start with
a wish for Sam.

He was playing pirates in the paddling pool.

"I'm Fairy Fizzwhizz," Phoebe announced.

"Tell me your wish and I'll make it come true!"

"Go away, pesky pixie, or you'll walk the
plank!" Sam growled.

"I'm not a pixie!" Phoebe stamped,
"now make a wish, or I'll bop you!"
"All right," Sam laughed. "I wish
I had a parrot."

Phoebe skipped happily through the garden.
"What shall I use to magic a parrot?"
she wondered . . .

. . . and there, on a leaf, she
spotted a ladybird.
"You'll make a perfect parrot!"
she said, and began her spell.

"*Ibb-bib-bob* ~
oh, do stay still!

"*Tip-tap-top* ~
stop flying!

"Oh you mean ladybird, come back!!!" she shouted, as it zoomed away.

"I'm not a very good fairy,"
Phoebe sighed to Mummy
and Daddy. "I can't fly, and
I can't magic a parrot."

"Never mind," said Daddy,
"we need some magic – you
can add fairy sprinkles to
the cakes for your birthday
tea – yummy!"

Phoebe made the cakes look so special,
she felt just like a fairy again.
"I'm going to tell Sam I really
can do magic!" she said.

But oh dear, poor Sam
was in a tizz. The mast
of his ship was snapped in two.
"It won't mend," he said sadly,
"now I can't be a pirate any more."

"Don't worry, I'll fix it!" said Phoebe.
"My magic's getting better.
I just needed practice!"

Phoebe twirled twice, then tapped the mast gently. Nothing happened.

She thought and thought.
   "I know," she said, "we'll close our eyes, and wish very hard."

Sam closed his eyes, but Phoebe tiptoed to the boat.
   "*One . . . two . . . three . . . fiddle-de-dee . . .*" she whispered.

"Ta-daaa!"

Sam opened his eyes . . . and saw a sparkling new mast on his pirate ship.

"You really can do magic, Fairy Fizzwhizz!" he laughed.

"I did, I did!" squealed Phoebe, and they sailed together until Daddy called, "Ahoy there, time for tea!"

Mummy and Daddy, Phoebe and Sam shared a fabulous fairy feast.

"I like being a fairy," yawned Phoebe, as the stars began to shine.

"You are a fantastic fairy," said Mummy, "but even fairies need their beds." And she carried Phoebe up to her fairy castle.

As Mummy kissed her goodnight,
Phoebe whispered in her ear:
"I didn't really do fairy magic,
Mummy."
　　"Oh yes you did," said Mummy.
"You were kind and thoughtful,
and you helped Sam feel
　　happy – I think that's the best
　　fairy magic in the world."

More sparkling books from Little Tiger Press!

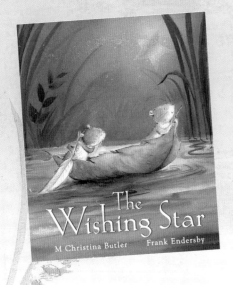

The Wishing Star

M Christina Butler • Frank Endersby

Noodle's Knitting

With soft-to-touch wool on every page

Sheryl Webster • Caroline Pedler

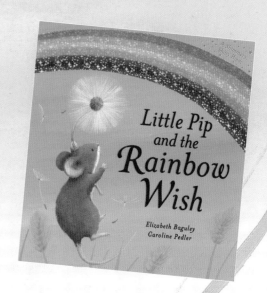

Little Pip and the Rainbow Wish

Elizabeth Baguley • Caroline Pedler

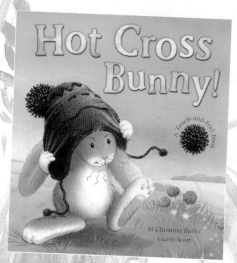

Hot Cross Bunny!

A Touch-and-Feel book

M Christina Butler • Gavin Scott

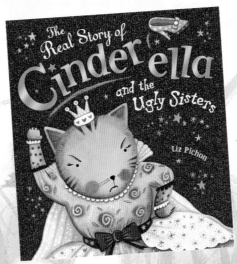

The Real Story of Cinderella and the Ugly Sisters

Liz Pichon

Little Friend

COLLEEN McKEOWN

For information regarding any of the above titles
or for our catalogue, please contact us:
Little Tiger Press, 1 The Coda Centre,
189 Munster Road, London SW6 6AW
Tel: 020 7385 6333 • Fax: 020 7385 7333
E-mail: info@littletiger.co.uk
www.littletigerpress.com